This book belongs to:

_____

I read it by myself on:

_____

The Tale of Tikky, the Quail

小鹌鹑蒂蒂的故事

Jenny Zhengyu Lin   文：林徵宇
Illustrated by Leo Li   圖：李裡奧

Washington Writers Press
Published in November 2021

華盛頓作家出版社
2021 年 11 月出版

It was a hot July 4ᵗʰ morning. Tikky, the quail, was standing facing a mirror. He was hatched for one week now. Daddy was working on a holiday project in town. Mummy was fast asleep after cleaning the nest. Tikky was looking at his wings in the mirror. "My wings are short," he thought. "How can I fly like the other birds?" Tikky longed for a flight.

一个炎热的七月四日早晨，小鹌鹑蒂蒂站在镜子前。他出壳一个星期了。爸爸在城里忙节日的活动。妈妈打扫完鹌巢后睡着了。小蒂蒂看着自己的翅膀想，"我的翅膀好短，怎么才能像别的鸟儿那样飞起来呢？"

The day before, Kikee, the jackrabbit had come. "There will be a July 4ᵗʰ parade at Virginia City," she said to Mrs. Quail. "Can Tikky come to watch the parade with me?"

"No, no," said Mrs. Quail. "Tikky is not ready to go outside of the village. He cannot fly across the strange roads."

"I can run fast," cried Tikky. "Let me go, please."

"Can't you wait after your daddy gives you a flying lesson?"

昨天，长耳兔侃侃来对鹌鹑妈妈说，"城里有庆祝国庆的游行。我想请蒂蒂和我一起去看。"鹌鹑太太说，"不行。他去不了。他还不会过马路呢"。蒂蒂叫道，"我可以的。让我去吧！"妈妈说，"等你爸爸教会你飞行再说吧。"

"You will miss the parade tomorrow,"
sighed Kikee, then she left.

侃侃叹了一口气，"你错过游行啰。"她走了。

Rustle, rustle. Tikky suddenly saw Kikee's long ears in the mirror as she popped into the room. "Tikky, this is Poppin, my friend." She pointed to a grey squirrel that had come with her. "He cannot fly, but he wants to go with me."

"Let's run together," smiled Poppin. He did not have wings, but a twitching fuzzy tail.

唦，侃侃的长耳朵出现在镜子里。她指着一只灰色的松鼠说，"蒂蒂，这是我的朋友啵啵。他也不会飞。可他想和我一块去。" 啵啵笑着说，"我们一起跑着去"。啵啵连翅膀都没有，只有一条蓬松的尾巴。

"*Yes!*" Tikky nodded with the teardrop-shaped feather bobbing on his head. He left a note on the mirror: "Mommy, I will go watch the parade with Kikee and Poppin." Then he ran off at his friends' sides.

蒂蒂甩动着头顶漂亮的珠形头羽欢呼，"*耶*！" 他留了张字条在镜子上，"妈咪，我和侃侃、啵啵一起去看游行了。"

Kikee had long legs. "Hurry up," shouted Kikee as she ran way ahead of Tikky and Poppin. "We don't want to miss the parade!"

侃侃的长腿奔跑在蒂蒂和啵啵前面。她大声喊着，"快点啊！我们别迟到了。"

Poppin ran after Kikee. Tikky ran after Poppin. Soon they passed through the grassland.

啵啵紧跟着侃侃。蒂蒂紧跟着啵啵。一会儿，他们跑过了大草坪。

"We need to cross that road quickly," Kikee pointed to a wide and busy road. She made three high jumps, then waved her long ears from the other side of the road.

侃侃指着一条极宽的大路说，"我们要穿越那条马路。"她高高地跃起三次，然后就在马路那一边晃动着她的长耳朵。

"I'm coming!" Poppin ran like a breeze, then waved his fuzzy tail from the other side of the road.

　"来啦！"啵啵像一阵风似地吹过，然后就在马路的那一边摇摆着他的毛尾巴。

A car was approaching as Tikky was just about to get on the road. The squealing noise of the brakes made him stop. "Fly, fly, fly over!" shouted Kikee and Poppin. Imagining his daddy, Tikky spread his two wings quickly and jumped into the air as high as he could.

Flap, flap, flap! Surprisingly, he flew above the road and landed next to Kikee, just as the car passed behind him like the wind.

蒂蒂正要跃上大路，一辆车飞驰而来。刺耳的轮胎摩擦声吓得蒂蒂停住了步子。侃侃和啵啵叫起来，"飞呀飞呀，飞过来！"蒂蒂不禁模仿着爸爸的样子，猛地打开左右翅膀使劲向空中跳起。

呼! 出乎蒂蒂意料，他飞过了大路，落在侃侃的旁边。那车在他身后呼啸而过。

"You made it!" shouted Kikee.
"Well done, Tikky!" cried Poppin.

侃侃叫道，"你过了！" 啵啵叫道，"好棒噢！"

"I can fly! Hurray!" shouted Tikky. He looped a loop. His head feather looped a loop.

"我会飞啦！"蒂蒂乐着转起了圈圈。漂亮的头羽也转着圈圈。

Now they were running in a bushy desert. The hot sun shined on the rocks and sand. "It's too hot！" said Poppin. "I am so thirsty."

他们继续在一大片遍布荆棘的沙漠上奔跑。太阳火辣辣的。啵啵说，"真热啊！我好渴！"

"There's a stream," pointed Kikee, as she jumped really high and looked ahead. "Behind that big red rock." She jumped high and crossed over the rock.

"那有一条小溪。 " 侃侃跳起来指着前方。 " 在那红岩石的后面。 " 说着，她奔向那块红色的大石头，一跃而过。

With a wink, Poppin climbed and disappeared behind the other side of the big red rock.

一眨眼，啵啵爬了上去，消失在大红石的后面。

"Wait! The rock is too high for me!" hollered
Tikky. "I can't see either of you!"

"Be brave!" shouted Kikee. The tips of her
ears were waving from the other side of the rock.

蒂蒂急了，"等等，这块石头太高了！我看不见你们！"
"勇敢点！"侃侃回应道。她的耳朵尖尖在石头的那一边摇
晃着。

"I'll try," said Tikky to himself. "Be brave!" He spread his two wings, took a deep breath, *Whoosh,* and flew over the red rock.

蒂蒂对自己说，"我要试一试！对，勇敢些！"他展开翅膀，深深呼了一口气，*咦呼*，竟然飞过了大红石头。

"You can fly higher than you thought!" shouted Kikee. She gave Tikky a big hug. "The water is sweet," said Poppin. "I feel great!"

侃侃赞道，"你可以飞得比你想得高勒！"她给了蒂蒂一个大大的拥抱。啵啵出现了，"水是甜的。我又有劲儿了！"

"I can fly like a REAL bird now! " Tikky thought proudly as he dipped his head feathers in the water to cool off. "How much farther do we have to go, Kikee?"

"Only 10 more minutes along this country road," answered Kikee, as she dipped her long ears in the water to cool off too.

蒂蒂一边把头羽浸到水里凉快一边高兴地想，"我可以像鸟儿一样飞了！"他问侃侃，"我们还要走多远？""沿着这条山道再走十来分钟。"侃侃一边把长耳朵浸到水里凉快一边回答。

Whirrrr! Every now and then, Tikky practiced his new flying skills.

"Look!" shouted Tikky, as he was in the air again. "There is a giant monster coming this way." A twisting smoke-colored monster was dancing upward. The closer it got, the taller it grew.

呀, 呀, 蒂蒂不时练习一下新的飞行方法。"看啊,"当他又一次在空中时叫了起来,"一只大怪物往这来了!"一个旋转飞快的烟黄色妖魔扭动着升向空中。越走近, 它越高大。

"Wow!" shouted Poppin. "It's a tornado!" He hid under a sage bush immediately and covered himself with the fuzzy tail.

　　"哇! 那是龙卷风吧!" 啵啵叫起来。他躲到一丛鼠尾草下面，用毛毛的大尾巴盖住了身体。

"Hahaha. It is not a tornado! It is called a Dust Devil. It picks up sand and debris," laughed Kikee. "But It's harmless! A Dust Devil is a whirlwind in extremely hot air."

"Really?" said Tikky, excited but still puzzled.

"I want to follow it and check it out." He ran towards the spinning monster. The Dust Devil moved straight up and was reaching the clouds quickly.

"哈哈，那不是龙卷风。那叫沙尘魔。它卷起沙子和尘屑。" 侃侃笑着说。"它是无害的。是由空气中特别热的气流旋转出来的。" "真的？" 蒂蒂兴奋地又好奇起来，"我想追过去看仔细点。" 他快步奔向旋转着的怪物。那沙尘魔向空中伸展，一下入了白云中。

As Tikky ran to the edge of the Dust Devil, Kikee made a big jump into the center of the monster. "Oh, no! Sand got in my eyes," cried Kikee. "I can't see".

蒂蒂快要触到沙尘魔的身躯时，侃侃一个大跳进入了沙尘魔的中央。"噢！我的眼睛进沙子了！我看不见了！"她嚷起来。

"Give me your hand!" shouted Tikky, as he took off and flew into the Dust Devil. Kikee grabbed his feet and dangled under him.

"One, two, three, jump up!" shouted Tikky. The minute Kikee was in the air, Tikky flew out of the Dust Devil and landed gently.

"手伸给我！"蒂蒂一边飞入旋转的沙尘魔，一边喊。侃侃抓到他的一只脚。两个一起随着旋流晃荡着。"一、二、三！跳！"蒂蒂大吼。侃侃在空中的那一瞬间，蒂蒂飞出了沙尘魔，轻轻降落在地上。

"You two really scared me," said Poppin, as the Dust Devil faded away. He helped Kikee clear her eyes.

"你俩吓坏我了！" 啵啵说。看着沙尘魔飞远了，他帮侃侃清洗了眼睛。

"Thank you, Tikky! Thank you, Poppin!" smiled Kikee. "Let's run quickly. "

"蒂蒂， 谢谢你！啵啵，谢谢你！我们快点走吧！" 侃侃开心地说。

They arrived in Virginia City just as the parade began. "Tikky, Kikee, Poppin!" Someone was calling.

Tikky saw his mommy and daddy. "We read your note and we came along too," smiled Mr. Quail.

"We saw you flying through the dust devil with Kikee," smiled Mrs. Quail.

"My wings are short, but I can fly when I need to!" Tikky said proudly as he got a big hug from his mommy and daddy.

他们到达市中心的时候，游行刚开始。"蒂蒂！侃侃！啵啵！"有人在远处喊。蒂蒂看见妈妈和爸爸。"看见你的字条，我们就来了。"鹌鹑爸爸笑着说。"我们看见你带着侃侃飞出了沙尘魔。"鹌鹑妈妈笑着说。蒂蒂自豪地说，"我的翅膀有点短，但在需要的时候我可以飞起来！"妈妈爸爸给了他一个大大的拥抱。

People and bands were marching, flags and balloons were flying.

"Happy July 4th!" shouted Kikee, as she waved her big ears.

"Happy July 4th!" shouted Poppin, as he waved his fuzzy tail.

"Happy July 4th!" shouted the Quail family, as they waved their dancing head feathers.

人们和乐队在前进。旗帜和气球在飘舞。"国庆快乐！"侃侃欢呼着，长长的耳朵左右晃着。"国庆快乐！" 啵啵欢呼着，毛毛的尾巴左右摇着。"国庆快乐！" 蒂蒂全家欢呼着，漂亮的头羽上下舞蹈着。

（完）

Do your own coloring

Made in the USA
Las Vegas, NV
17 April 2022